PAUL KROPP

HOT CARS

Editorial development and production: Sandra Gulland
Design: Artplus/Brant Cowie
Illustrations: Tina Holdcroft

EMC Publishing, St. Paul, Minnesota

Library of Congress Cataloging in Publication Data

Kropp, Paul.
  Hot cars.

  (Encounter series / Paul Kropp)
  Summary: A teenager faces the consequences of his decision to buy a s
Corvette from professional car thieves.
  [1. Crime and criminals—Fiction]. I. Collins, Heather, ill. II. 7
III. Series: Kropp, Paul. Encounters series.

PZ7.K93Ho   [Fic]   81-5358

ISBN 0-88436-820-3   AACR2

Encounters Series Titles:

Burn Out	Fair Play
Dead On	Hot Cars
Dirt Bike	No Way
Dope Deal	Runaway

Published by EMCParadigm Publishing
875 Montreal Way
St. Paul, Minnesota 55102

Printed in the United States of America
0   9

CONTENTS

4

CHAPTER

1

Robert steered the old Ford pickup truck through piles of twisted and rusting cars. He could see the old wrecks all around him. There was a Mustang with no doors, a Chevy without a bumper, the front end of a big Olds Cutlass sitting on top of a rusty van. He drove the truck slowly through the wrecks and looked for the Pinto he needed.

Robert finally spotted the smashed Pinto over by the north fence of the junkyard. He stopped the truck near the car and climbed down from the cab. Then he flipped his metal braces, the crutches he needed to walk, from behind the seat. He used them to swing himself over to the Pinto.

Robert lifted the hood to see if the distributor was still in place. He was in luck. He began to remove the part with two wrenches he kept in his jeans. Ten minutes later, he pulled the whole distributor out of the engine.

He started to bring the part back to his truck when he saw his friend Dave walking toward him. The watchdog at the north fence started barking like crazy.

"Why do those dogs always have to bark at me?" Dave shouted.

"Because you look like somebody who'd steal hubcaps from his own grandmother," Robert called out with a grin. "What are you getting for your Camaro today?"

"What makes you think I came out here just to get another part for my car?" Dave asked.

"The screwdriver you're carrying gives you away. You're not carrying it for fun," Robert said with a laugh.

Robert's friend Dave had been working on an old Camaro for over a year. When he first bought the car for $700, it looked like it should be sitting in the junkyard with all the other wrecks. But Dave and Robert had put enough paint, Bondo and prayer into the car to make the Camaro look pretty good. With a little more engine work, Dave planned to resell the car for more than $2000. Then he could go after the car he really wanted—a Corvette.

"All I need is a headlight," Dave explained. "I was driving along Santa Monica yesterday when the low beam burned out. Your father says I can have a new light for free."

"That's got to be the first thing Crazy Phil ever gave away. He's so cheap he wouldn't offer to buy a round of drinks at an AA meeting." Robert smiled at his own joke. "Is he still working on the other truck?"

"No, he was just sitting around reading the paper and drinking coffee when I left him."

Robert shrugged. If his father put as much time into the junk business as he did into coffee and newspapers they might make a little money with the yard. As it was, Robert just looked down at his ripped jeans and shook his head.

"Your neighbors are moving up in the world," Dave said. He was staring between two slats of the wooden fence.

Robert swung over next to him to see what was happening at the warehouse next door. "That's a Jaguar, isn't it? I think my father may have to get a new truck just to keep up with the neighbors," Robert said with a laugh.

"It's a Jaguar XJS," Dave said. "Sometimes I wonder if a $25 000 car like that would really be any faster than my Corvette, when I get it."

Robert tried to imagine Dave sitting in a Corvette. Then he shook his head and went back to the old pickup truck. He knew that Dave had been dreaming of a Corvette for years, just waiting for his chance to get hold of one. When every other kid in Los Angeles was still putting his money into baseball cards and bubble gum, Dave was dreaming about Cragar knock-off wheels and L-88 heads. Now that he was in his last year of high school, Dave probably was a lot closer to

the real thing.

"I can tell by that grin on your face that you don't believe me," Dave said. "But I'm working on a deal right now that will get rid of that patched-up Camaro and put me on the street in a 'Vette. You just wait—the Blue Goose will eat my dust."

"The Blue Goose is getting hungry just waiting for that dust," Robert said while patting his special truck. The old Ford pickup had been fixed up by Robert's father so that he could drive it without having to use his legs. A special throttle in the Blue Goose gave gas to the engine and Robert could use the hand brake to stop the truck. The Blue Goose wasn't safe enough to drive on the street but Robert loved to ride around the junkyard in it.

Robert watched as Dave unscrewed two headlights from the Pinto and carried them carefully back to the truck. Robert looked at him as if to ask why he had taken both.

"I'll be lucky if even one of them works," Dave explained. "With my luck, maybe I should take four or five back."

"You sound like a guy who plays hide-and-seek and nobody looks for him. If you'll stop moaning and groaning like a loser, I'll drive you back," Robert offered.

"I'll shut up and take the ride," Dave said as he climbed into the cab next to Robert.

In a short while they had driven back to the office where Robert's father ran the junkyard. A sign next to the door read, *Nuts and Bolts, Auto Parts, the biggest supply in Los Angeles*.

Most of the sign was a lie. Phil wasn't really crazy, he didn't stock any new auto parts, and his junkyard wasn't even close to the largest in Los Angeles. But Phil always said that people can take the truth only a little at a time. "If you give them too much, they'll either stone you to death or make you a hero," he used to add.

Robert pulled the truck to a stop beside the small office at the front of the junkyard.

"Where is he?" Robert asked.

Dave shrugged and looked around the room. There were the usual piles of brake

11

The sign reads:

Nuts and Bolt
Auto Parts
the biggest
supply in
Los Angeles

12

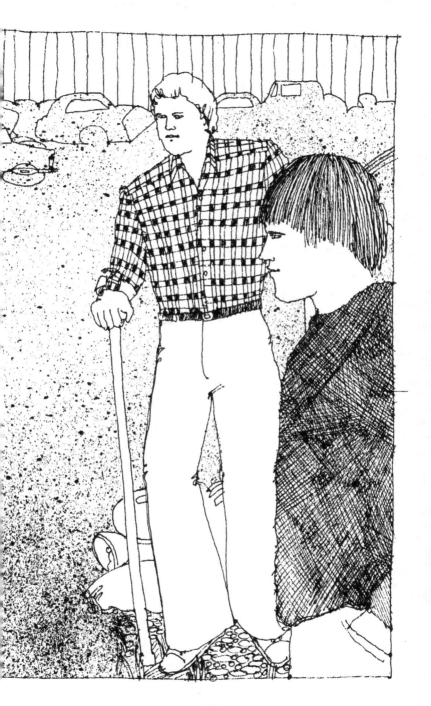

drums, hubs and tire jacks. Off in the corner stood a wood-burning stove and the rusty Dodge truck that Crazy Phil liked to use. But neither of them could see Robert's father.

"Dad, where are you?" Robert called out into the piles of junk.

"Uunh."

They heard a groan come from the direction of the old Dodge. Dave ran to see where the voice had come from. He stopped dead when he saw Crazy Phil's legs sticking out from beneath the truck.

CHAPTER 2

"Dad, what's the matter?"

Robert's father slid from underneath the truck and sat up, staring at the boys. His face was covered with grease and he smelled as sweet as an Arco station. The grey-haired man wiped his face on the sleeve of his workcoat and then grinned.

"I have hit upon the *essence* of the problem," Crazy Phil said.

"What are you talking about?" Dave asked.

"It's a joke, son, to quote the famous fowl Foghorn Leghorn. *L'essence* is French for gasoline and the problem with this rusty Dodge here is in the gas tank," he explained.

"So you know why the truck stopped working?" Robert asked.

"The problem was really quite simple —mud. In fact, when I unscrewed the gas tank drain plug the problem hit me right in the face. It was like saying, here's mud in your eye," Crazy Phil laughed at his own joke.

"Would you stop the dumb jokes and try to make sense," Robert said, getting angry with his father. "You mean that somebody tried to sabotage the truck?"

"I didn't say sabotage. I just said that there was some mud and water in the gas tank. When I tried to start the truck this morning, the mud clogged up the fuel pump so the engine wouldn't fire. I just cleaned out the gas tank. Maybe you two can help me with the rest of the job," Phil said, looking at Robert and Dave.

Robert stared at his father wondering how the old man could keep on smiling after something like this. The trouble with Crazy Phil was that he never stopped smiling, no matter what people did to him. Robert remembered the time

a farmer came in to get an engine for his pickup truck and said he'd pay Crazy Phil in turkeys. Did Crazy Phil use his head and say no? No way!

For three months the junkyard was filled with the noise and smell of a hundred turkeys. Crazy Phil kept on smiling even when the turkeys started dying from the heat of the summer sun. Then he shrugged and said the dying turkeys made him feel good about people. "At least people know enough to get out of the sun and into the shade," he'd say. "I've known stupid people but nobody as stupid as these turkeys." That was Robert's father.

"Dad, who would want to put mud into your gas tank? You've got to be serious about this for a minute."

"I got serious once in 1944 and it scared me so much I haven't tried it since." Crazy Phil winked at Dave. "For all I know it could have been anybody. So there's no sense getting mad at the whole world. You young kids may think I'm crazy for smiling all the time, but it sure beats looking like you suck lemons for a living. Right Dave?"

Robert looked over at his friend. He noticed that Dave's mouth was shaped as if he really did suck lemons all day long.

Crazy Phil went ahead without waiting for Dave to answer. "Remember that old saying I told you about, 'Not all show teeth mean laugh.' I may be smiling about this whole thing, but that doesn't mean I'm not worried about it."

"You're wild, Phil," Dave said with a laugh. "I'll never know for sure if you're a genius or just crazy. . . ."

Dave's words were cut off when a customer came through the front door. This set off enough bells and buzzers to drown out any talking in the office. Crazy Phil had wired the door to wake him up if any customers came in. Robert thought that the noise was so loud it just drove customers away. The poor guy at the door look scared to death while Phil ran up front to close the door and shut off the noise.

During the war, before Robert was born, Crazy Phil had done well in the junk business. Scrap metal prices were high and people fixed up their cars instead of buying new ones. Robert used to hear his father talk about the old days. He once had eight men working for him and big plans to expand the yard.

Then Crazy Phil's luck seemed to go bad. The price for scrap metal fell and people stopped coming in to buy parts for their old cars. Robert was born with a spine problem that meant he needed braces to help him walk. Then Robert's mother died and Crazy Phil seemed to fall apart. For a while it looked like he was trying to live up to his nickname. But Phil pulled out of the slump. He came back and greeted the world with a smile that was wise and wild at the same time.

"What did the customer want?" Robert asked.

"He just needed some hubcaps for an Austin Mini. I told him he could go out and look around because we don't have any in here."

Robert's father climbed back under the truck again to screw the drain plug back into the gas tank. Robert sat down next to him and handed him the tools he needed while Dave went out front to put a headlight in his Camaro.

It was pretty quiet for five minutes while the three of them worked. Then the customer came back in from the yard.

"Did you find your hubcaps?" Robert called out.

"No luck, I'm afraid. But you should look after your dogs a little better. The one out by the fence over there seems like he's pretty sick," the man said, pointing out the door.

Robert's father sat up and looked out into the junkyard. A second later, the old man was running toward the north fence with Dave and Robert trying to keep up.

When Robert finally caught up with his father he saw the whole story at a glance. The customer had been only half right. The German shepherd wasn't sick —he was dead.

CHAPTER
3

"Buddy, they killed you," Robert heard his father say.

The old man was bending over the dead body of the dog, rocking back and forth on his knees. There were no tears on his cheeks, though he might have felt better if he was able to cry. He rocked in silence, holding back any sign of his feelings.

Robert came up behind his father and looked down at the dead watchdog. Buddy had been the last pup in a litter born when Robert was still a child. Robert watched his father rocking on his

knees, but couldn't think of anything to do or say.

"Looks like he was a pretty old watchdog," Dave said quietly.

"Yeah," Robert answered. "We raised him from a puppy. He must be at least ten and that's pretty old for a dog."

"Like being seventy, they say." Dave finished Robert's thought.

"Come on, dad. You might as well get up and call the Humane Society," Robert said, trying to help the old man to his feet.

When Crazy Phil stood up, both Robert and Dave were surprised by the look on his face. It wasn't a look of grief so much as a look of anger. The old man's fists were tightened into balls and the skin of his forehead was tight.

"What's the matter?" Dave asked.

"Buddy didn't die of old age," Crazy Phil said slowly, not smiling at all.

"You don't think somebody killed him?" Robert asked.

His father didn't answer. Crazy Phil swept the ground with his eyes looking for some clue to explain the dog's death. Over near the Pinto, he found it.

"Look over there," Phil said, pointing at a piece of meat on the ground.

Robert went over with Dave to look at the meat. He could smell it when he got up close. It had a rotten stench that made him want to vomit, but that didn't mean anything in itself.

"Didn't you put this out for him?" Robert asked.

"No, but I have some idea who did," Crazy Phil said. Then he turned on his heel and walked back toward the store.

"Pretty strange," Dave said, shaking his head.

"Put this together with the mud in the gas tank, and it begins to look like something is happening around here. But I don't know enough just yet to make any sense of it all," Robert said.

"And it might mean nothing at all. You know, your dad is always saying that we're too serious about things," Dave said, trying to smile.

"Only this time Crazy Phil is as serious as we are," Robert said firmly.

Robert walked Dave back to his Camaro and waved him off. Dave kept hinting at some big deal he had set up for five o'clock. But Robert knew that Dave's big deals were about as solid as a house of cards.

The office was quiet for a Saturday afternoon. There was only one guy at the counter when Robert got back. All he wanted was a Chevy tail light. Robert saw that his father was already out front talking to another customer, some short guy in a big Cadillac.

Robert rang up the money for the tail light and sat down on a stool. He was waiting for the tow truck driver to come in. Then Robert could go out and drive around the yard for a while. He waited at the counter for forty minutes, but the guy never did show up.

Robert wondered why his father was still talking to the guy with a Cadillac out in front of the store. He thought for a while that Crazy Phil was just busy telling him stories or boring him with stupid jokes. Robert decided he should go outside to help the little guy out. After all, he said to himself, this was a junk business and not the corner tavern.

As soon as Robert got outside, he could tell that the two men were not having a friendly talk. They both shut up when Robert came out the door. The two men stared at him as he walked toward them.

"Robert, go back inside and take care of the counter," Crazy Phil yelled.

"I just came out to see if you wanted me to get anything."

"Go back and take care of the counter," Phil yelled again. This time he said it in a deeper voice that made his words an order.

Robert flipped his braces about and went back into the office, wondering

what was going on. He watched his father making wide gestures with his hands. The other man just stood there while Crazy Phil waved his arms. He was a short guy but seemed really powerful as if he had been a midget wrestler. The man kept nodding his head and never lost his cool.

Robert could tell by then that their talk had nothing to do with auto parts. He walked over to the door and opened it just a crack. He couldn't hear what the short guy was saying, but he could hear Phil yelling back at him, "You rats... I will never... Baxter, you and your people are rats... I know you did it... get out of here!"

With these last words, the little man spun around and climbed into his Cadillac. Crazy Phil went over to the car window and listened to something Robert couldn't hear. Then the car sped away and Crazy Phil was left alone in front of the office.

Robert stood behind the counter and waited for his father to come back inside the office. He didn't know if his father would want to talk but decided to ask

him anyway. Crazy Phil came bursting through the door.

"What's going on?" Robert asked.

"I'm not sure I know or even if I want to know. The older I get and the crazier I get, Robert, the less I want to know about. But I can tell you this. When the world dumps a real problem on you and you just have to answer it, then your answer has got to be the right one. It's got to be an answer you can live with—or maybe even die for."

With that, the old man shook his head and walked out into the junkyard.

CHAPTER 4

Robert sat outside his house waiting for Dave to come pick him up in the Camaro. His mind was still playing with the events of the day as if they were pieces in a puzzle he couldn't fit together.

He knew one watchdog was dead, the Dodge truck had been sabotaged and his father was in some kind of trouble. Robert told himself that these might be just accidents. But no accident would explain the rotten meat near the dog or the dirt in the gas tank.

Crazy Phil was the key piece in the puzzle, Robert said to himself. His father wouldn't talk at all about the short man in the Cadillac. Robert had asked him about the man again at dinner time, but Crazy Phil had just put him off. The old man started to talk about famous people who died in stupid ways, like Claudius of Rome choking on a feather or Alexander the Great going under from a two-day drunk. Robert just couldn't get his father to talk about the strange events of the day.

Dave pulled up in his Camaro and cut short Robert's thoughts. Robert flipped his braces into the back and settled in the car.

"Where are we going?" Robert asked.

"Thought we might go for a ride downtown. Maybe we'll stop at Pershing Square and hang around for a while. I've had a big day and there are a couple of things I want to talk about."

The Camaro zoomed along Highway 101 while Dave tuned in KRCY on the radio. Robert could see that his friend was upset about something but he didn't know what the problem was. The strange events of the day might bother Dave a little, but they really weren't his problems. Robert wondered when Dave would talk about what was on his mind.

"Well?"

"Well what?" Dave answered.

"Well, what did you want to talk about, you dummy?"

"I don't know if I should discuss the whole thing with you or not. I need some advice on what to do, but I already know what you'll say. And if I know all that, why should I talk to you at all?" Dave said as if talking to himself.

"So let me out at the first bus stop and you can work it out yourself," Robert said, only half-kidding.

"What I mean is that I've already made my decision but have to talk to someone about it. I've got this chance to pick up a Corvette for only $3000 if I act on it quick enough," Dave explained.

"At that price, the car must be ready to fall apart. Have you seen it?" Robert asked.

"Not yet. I have to agree to the deal without seeing the car first, if you understand what I'm saying. The problem isn't that the car is in rotten shape . . . the problem is that it's hot."

"Black market?"

"You're absolutely right. You've got the picture. I heard about this guy named Baxter who sells really expensive cars for less than half what they're worth. He only handles cars like Jaguars, Corvettes and Cadillacs. I don't know for sure where the cars come from or what he does to them, but people say they can't be traced back by the police," Dave explained.

"I've heard about big car-theft gangs that can get away with that. But why do you have to buy from those guys?" Robert asked.

"Because they can get me a Corvette for half the price I'd have to pay anyone else. You know better than anybody how much I want a Corvette. It makes my mouth water just to think about owning the car."

"Stop drooling and tell me about the deal," Robert said.

"I talked to the guy this afternoon and he says he's got a '75 Corvette with a 350 engine and side-pipes for $3000, cash. If I can sell my Camaro this week, that'll give me $2000 and I can borrow

the rest from my brother," Dave said. He pulled the car off the highway onto Macy Street.

"You're taking a big chance, you know," Robert warned. "You haven't even seen the car and you don't know anything about these guys in the gang. You don't really know if the police will finally trace the car and take it back."

"I knew you wouldn't like the idea."

"It's not just a stupid idea, it's the whole business that bothers me. It's too easy to say I'll break the law just this once to get what I really want. After the first time, there's no telling when it will stop."

"Stop making such a big deal out of this. It's really nothing more than a way to buy a great car, a car I've always wanted, cheap. You keep on trying to make this seem worse than it is. You act like I was going out knocking over little old ladies for pocket money," Dave said.

"Yeah, but I want you to see the connection between buying a hot car and the whole business of car theft in the U.S. Today you're going in on one end of the business. Tomorrow it may be your car that's stolen," Robert said, taking a breath. "My father was saying this afternoon that sometimes the world dumps a big problem on you. He says the decision you make has got to be one you can live with. I think he's right."

"And I think that's just Crazy Phil mouthing off when he should be taking care of his junkyard. I said this afternoon that I didn't know if he was a genius or a fool. Now I've got an idea which way it goes," Dave growled.

"That's enough. Stop the car and let me out right here," Robert said firmly.

"You've got to be crazy too. We're nowhere near a bus stop so how are you going to get home?" Dave asked.

"I can take care of myself better than you might think. Just because I walk on crutches doesn't mean I have to sit here while you bad-mouth my father. Now pull over," Robert ordered.

Dave steered the Camaro over to the curb and let Robert get out. Robert struggled for a minute to get his metal braces in place after he left the car.

"Have you made a decision on this deal?" Robert yelled through the window.

40

He was still mad about what Dave had said but he hoped there was time for his friend to change his mind.

"Look in the paper tomorrow and you'll see," Dave answered. Then he raced away from the curb.

CHAPTER
5

1976 Camaro, PS, PB, KONI's, Holley carb, Goodrich T/A's, fine street machine, clean. Call 449-3232.

Robert put down the Sunday paper and saw that Dave had made his decision before even talking to him. That meant Saturday night was a waste. He had called a taxi after getting out of Dave's car and gone to the closest bus stop. Their argument in the car had cost him a three buck cab fare and his best friend.

"Let's go over to the yard," Crazy Phil yelled upstairs.

"On Sunday?"

"If you want to sit around the house like a roll of wet toilet paper, that's your business. I'm going over to the yard and thought you might like to come along."

Robert didn' know why Crazy Phil would go to the junkyard on Sunday unless he was worried about more sabotage. Robert thought he had better be with his father if there was going to be trouble.

Crazy Phil drove the old Dodge truck so fast that Robert thought the old man had really snapped. He braked the truck to a stop in front of the *Nuts and Bolts* sign. Then he raced into the office before Robert could even get out of the truck.

When Robert got into the office, he saw his father was listening for something.

"What is it?" Robert asked.

"It's not what I hear, it's what I don't hear. I had a feeling that something had happened."

Robert shut up and listened for a minute. Then he realized what was missing—the watchdogs weren't barking. Robert listened again but all he could hear was the wind blowing through the wrecked cars.

Crazy Phil was already out the rear door running toward the east fence. Robert saw him run across the yard and then stop dead.

Robert swung himself out of the office but slowed just outside the rear door. From where he stood, he could see the curled-up shape of the dog.

Crazy Phil stopped by the dead dog for a few seconds and then ran over to where his last watchdog was chained. He found the body of the other dog lying in the mud.

When Robert finally caught up with his father, the old man was standing perfectly still near the body of the second dog.

"They got the last two," Crazy Phil said, almost without any feeling.

"Yeah."

"There was no reason to kill these two. After they killed Buddy yesterday, I knew they were serious," Phil cried.

"Who are you talking about?" Robert asked.

Crazy Phil looked at Robert for a few

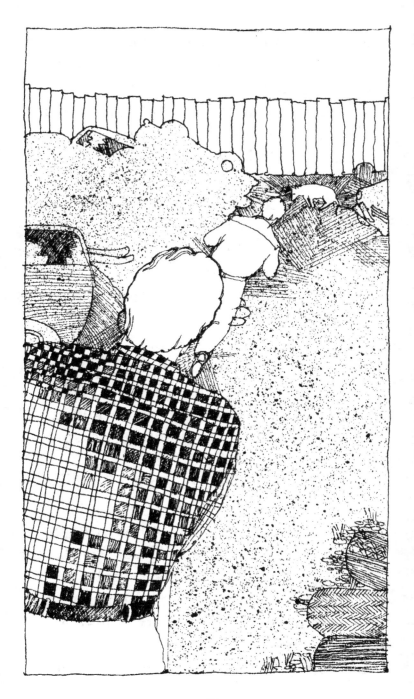

seconds trying to decide what he would tell him. He opened his mouth as if searching for the right words.

"Do you remember that man I was talking to yesterday, the guy in the Cadillac?" Phil began. "He came to me last week with some sort of deal. He wanted to expand his warehouse over there so he said he'd give me $80 000 for the junkyard. He'd even let me work for him after he bought me out."

"But you've never wanted to sell the business," Robert cut in.

"I know I haven't talked about it much. But that doesn't mean the thought hasn't come into this old skull of mine. Business isn't very good, you know, and I guess I wouldn't mind selling to somebody," Phil explained.

"But what does that have to do with dogs and the truck?"

"I said I wouldn't mind selling to somebody. I didn't say I'd sell to Baxter, the little guy. There was something about him I didn't like right from the start. When I said no to the deal, he started trying to force me into it. You know how I am when somebody tries to force me into something," Phil said, looking at Robert.

"Like a mule."

"Right. So he starts telling me that little accidents might start happening around here."

"You should go to the police before he does any more. He can't get away with stuff like that," Robert said.

"But I don't have any proof to show them. I've got three dead dogs and a tray full of dirty gasoline. There's nobody to prove that I ever talked to Baxter and nothing to connect him to what's happened. I've had it," Phil groaned.

"But you can't just give in to them," Robert said.

"I didn't say I was giving in. I'm still working out an idea of what to do. Give me a little time to think and I'll talk to you about it."

Robert felt angry as he watched his father walking back to the shop. Crazy Phil was stooping like a beaten and confused old man, not like the man Robert knew his father to be.

Robert stayed near the fence for a few minutes getting more and more angry about the whole thing. He decided to drive the Blue Goose around the yard while he tried to figure out what to do.

The driving helped to calm him down. It made him think about problems close at hand, like steering the truck, instead of big problems he couldn't deal with. He drove around the junkyard for a good half hour. Then he stopped the truck near the wrecked Pinto and sat on the running board. He traced the letters that spelled Blue Goose with his finger.

Robert got as far as the "u" when he heard a car drive up to the warehouse

next door. He went over to the fence to have a better look just as the car horn sounded and the metal garage door opened. Robert hurried to the space in the fence in time to see a black Cadillac drive into the warehouse.

It must be Baxter, Robert said to himself. He kept his eye fixed on the warehouse, trying to see what was inside. There seemed to be a couple of cars besides the Cadillac, but it was hard to make out any details. A few seconds later the garage door lowered back down. Robert leaned back against the trunk of the Pinto and tried to sort things out.

A voice broke into his thoughts, "Are you some sort of peeping Tom?"

CHAPTER
6

Robert wheeled around, not sure who was standing behind him. His blood raced for a second until he saw his friend Dave standing on the other side of the Pinto.

"Take it easy, Robert. I was only making a joke. Why? Can't you take a joke?"

"I'm glad to see that you have a sense of humor but that doesn't change what I think about the Corvette deal. I saw your ad in the paper this morning and just hope you don't get any calls from it," Robert said.

"I don't think we'll ever agree on the

deal, so why don't we just drop it. Like my mother says, we can agree to disagree and still be friends."

Robert saw a smile come to Dave's face that made him feel bad about giving his friend such a hard time. There wasn't any point in talking any more about the deal. Robert had explained what he thought about it and Dave had made his decision. The real question was whether they could stay friends in spite of the problem.

"O.K., we'd better drop it. The real problem is right here in the junkyard and Crazy Phil may need our help. When we got here this morning, we found the other two watchdogs dead," Robert whispered.

"But Crazy Phil didn't say anything to me," Dave said, his mouth falling open.

"He's so confused right now I'm surprised he didn't say 'Good night' when you came in. The guy who owns that warehouse over there wants to buy out Crazy Phil's junkyard. My father said he didn't want to sell and the guy started to use strong-arm stuff. That's when they put mud in the Dodge truck and began killing the dogs," Robert said.

"It sounds like they're going to keep up the sabotage until Crazy Phil gives up," Dave said. "But that doesn't make much sense. Nothing personal, but why would anybody want to take over a crummy junkyard like this? The whole thing just doesn't add up."

"That's what doesn't make any sense. It could be that they plan to expand the warehouse and need some of this land for building. But why would they use sabotage for that? There's got to be something else behind all this." Dave stopped talking when he heard the sound of a car on the other side of the fence.

"You see, we're not the only ones who come in to work on Sunday," Robert said, swinging over to the fence.

Through broken boards in the old fence, Robert and Dave watched the warehouse. The big black Cadillac had pulled out onto the gravel driveway. One of the men from the car went to pull on a chain to bring down the garage door. Then he left the warehouse through a side door and climbed back in the car. A second later, the Cadillac pulled away

from the warehouse and it was quiet again.

"What kind of business do you think they're running in that place?" Dave asked.

"I couldn't see very much inside. It looks like there are more cars and some benches to work on. There's a big, shiny thing, too, like something I've seen at school." Robert tried to think.

"Like what?" Dave asked.

"It looked like those big arc lamps they use in the auto body shop at school to bake the paint on cars. Hey, maybe the warehouse is being used as a body shop."

Robert and Dave were both silent for a minute, still trying to piece together the puzzle. If the place was a body shop, why was there no sign and why would it need to take over the junkyard? If it wasn't a body shop, what kind of business was it?

"If we could get a look inside, we could probably figure out this whole thing," Dave said with a sigh.

"Maybe we can," Robert said while looking carefully at the building.

The warehouse was built of cement blocks and had two big garage doors. The door the men had used was the smaller of the two. The larger garage door was a wooden one, big enough to let a truck inside. There were also two small fire doors, covered with sheet metal, at the sides of the building. All the windows were covered over with chain-link fencing.

"The place is built like a fort," Dave said with a groan.

"I think I see a way in if you're good at climbing," Robert said. "But we'd better check to make sure there's nobody inside. If these guys will kill Crazy Phil's dogs, I bet they'd enjoy busting our knees."

Robert and Dave pulled a slat out of the fence and walked slowly toward the warehouse. They weren't worried too much because no windows were facing them. When they got close to the metal garage door, Robert picked up a rock and handed it to Dave.

"What do you want me to do with this?" Dave whispered.

"Whip it at the door."

"What if somebody comes running out after us?"

"Then we walk slowly back to the junkyard like this is a Sunday stroll in Beverly Hills. There's no place to hide so we'll just have to risk it," Robert explained.

Dave thought about the plan for a minute and then nodded. He threw the rock against the metal door. The clank made a sound like thunder.

"Now walk slowly and we'll see what happens," Robert said, his voice shaking only a little.

CHAPTER

7

Nothing happened. Robert and Dave waited and listened hard for any sound inside the warehouse. It was dead quiet.

"So what's your plan for getting a look inside there?" Dave asked.

"We grab hold of that fence over the windows and climb up to the open window near the roof."

"That's quite a climb!" Dave said, looking up.

"You may not have arms as strong as mine, but you can use your feet. It should be as easy as climbing the playground fence at school," Robert said.

They walked over to the side of the warehouse and stared at the open window some twelve feet up off the ground. Robert started climbing first and had very little trouble. His strong arms carried him up the chain-link fence while his braces dangled from their safety straps.

Dave had to work harder to make the climb but he was soon hanging on to the fence right next to Robert. The open window was tilted out away from the others. It had an opening just big enough to let them climb through.

"Can you see anything?" Dave panted.

"Not very much. I'll climb in and sit on the window sill," Robert said moving toward the open window.

Robert was able to ease his body through the opening and sit on the sill while holding on to the fencing outside. He shifted his body sideways to get a better look inside and suddenly he lost control. He struggled for a second to keep his balance on the window sill. Then he fell into the warehouse.

"Robert, are you all right?" Dave yelled into the window.

Dave was afraid Robert would be too hurt to answer. But when he listened, all he could hear was laughing.

"What on earth are you laughing about?" Dave asked as he balanced his body in the open window.

"I fell right onto this old car seat under the window. Let yourself drop down—it's like falling on a mattress," Robert called up.

Dave waited for a minute. He was afraid of the height and not really sure he wanted to jump. But he couldn't leave his friend down there alone. He let go his grip and fell down into the darkness.

A dull thud sounded in the warehouse as Dave hit the car seat. His weight ripped the cloth cover and sent pieces of foam flying through the air.

When Robert's eyes could see in the dim light, he started moving through the warehouse. The first thing he saw was a row of cars—a Jaguar, a Porsche and a Corvette. The Jaguar was halfway into a new paint job and looked like it was having some body work. The Porsche was up on a hoist and Robert couldn't tell what was being done to it. The Corvette

was just sitting at the side, the chrome from its side-pipes glowing in the dim light.

On a bench near him, Robert saw a bunch of license plates from across the U.S. He looked back at the three cars and saw that only the Corvette had plates from California.

"Hey, Robert, look at this," Dave called to him from across the warehouse.

Robert moved over to him and saw he was holding a glass bottle in one hand.

"What have you got there?"

"Acid—just like in the Chemistry Lab at school."

Dave poured some of the acid on a piece of metal sitting on the bench. The acid started bubbling away until it left a pitted piece of metal behind.

"That's pretty strong stuff," Robert whistled.

"I've got a hunch I know what they do with the acid, too. Let's go over and look at that Corvette," Dave said.

Dave opened up the hood of the car and started looking around inside. A minute later he called to Robert, "Come look at this."

Robert stuck his head under the hood trying to see what Dave was pointing to.

"Look at that chassis ID plate, right there. Do you see those rivets that hold it onto the body of the car? They're the wrong kind. When a Corvette comes from the factory it has little rosettes on the rivets that hold the chassis ID plate to the car. Someone has switched the plate on this one."

"So it all makes sense," Robert said as he pulled his head out from under the hood. "The acid, the switched ID plates, the license plates from all over—this warehouse must be the center for a car-theft gang."

Robert knew that Los Angeles was one of the major cities for car theft. A gang could steal a car in San Francisco or San Diego and have it driven to Los Angeles the same night. Then the gang would fix the car so it couldn't be traced. They'd use acid to eat away the ID numbers and stamp new ones in place. Sometimes they'd repaint the car or change a few small parts. Then they'd make up some fake ownership papers and deliver the car for half what it was worth.

"I think you're probably right," Dave agreed. "And I've got a hunch about this Corvette. . . ."

Before Dave could finish explaining his hunch, they heard a car pull up outside the garage door.

CHAPTER

8

The garage door opened and a black Cadillac drove into the warehouse. Two men got out of the car. The taller one was dressed in a dark business suit. He looked around for a minute before talking to the short, powerful man on the other side of the car.

"Baxter, how do you turn on the lights in this place?"

"The switch is over there in the corner," Baxter yelled back while closing the garage door.

"Look at this crud all over the floor, will you? It looks like your guys have been playing kangaroo on top of this car seat." The man laughed as he turned on the overhead lights.

"You can't get good people to work any more, Frank," Baxter answered. "Sometimes I think these kids are as much trouble as that old guy at the junkyard next door."

Robert and Dave were hiding in the supply room while Baxter complained about Crazy Phil. Robert looked around and tried to figure out how much trouble they were in. The supply room was full of tools, nuts, bolts and other small auto parts. It also had a coffee machine whose "ready" light was glowing. Robert figured that it was only a matter of time until he and Dave would be caught. One of the men would soon want either a tool or some coffee from the machine.

"You can tell Marcel," Baxter said, "that I've got a buyer for the Corvette. I'm just waiting for the kid to come up with the money. That should give us enough time to make up new ownership papers to match the new ID numbers."

"Marcel doesn't care about any one

car, Baxter. He's worried about this whole thing with the junkyard. You've got to have some sort of cover when you're dealing in hot cars and a junkyard would be perfect. Without some real business for a front, the police will close you down before the year's out. This warehouse may be great for doing the work, but you need that junkyard to keep people from asking questions."

"Frank, I told you that I'm working on the old man. We got his dogs the other day and his truck the day before that. He's got to crack sooner or later," Baxter said.

"Marcel's a very important man, you know. When you get that big, you have a lot more money than time. I think he's starting to wonder about all these delays. If I were you, I'd send a couple of your boys to convince the old man real quick," Frank said, pounding his fists together.

"I get the message, Frank. Do you want a cup of coffee before we get your Porsche off the hoist?" Baxter asked.

Robert caught his breath in the supply room. He felt his heart beating faster and tried to calm down. He had to

decide what to do if Frank or Baxter opened the supply room door. He could probably knock out one of them with a smack from his metal braces, but that would still leave the other waiting outside.

"No, I just had a cup at lunch so I'll wait a while," Frank answered.

Robert stopped holding his breath and relaxed a little. He could feel Dave standing next to him and knew that his friend was scared, too. Frank's answer had given them some time to work on a way out of the supply room, but not much time. Robert looked around the dark room trying to find another door or maybe someplace to hide. It was hopeless. There was only one way out and that led to Baxter and Frank. The cabinets and boxes wouldn't even hide a large goldfish.

Out in the warehouse, Frank lowered the Porsche from the hoist and looked at its seats.

"Look at this real leather, Baxter. You don't come across a car like this very often. If you can get that junkyard business fixed up, maybe Marcel will give you a little present too."

"This car shows that you're moving up in the business," Baxter smiled.

"Marcel always takes care of the people who do good work for him, Baxter. Just remember that. Now get me the ownership papers and I'll be on my way."

"I got the papers ready in the supply room, it'll just take me a second. . . ."

Baxter was walking toward the supply room when he heard the first knock on the warehouse door. He stopped. The two men stared at each other and then the knock came again.

"Who's that?" Frank asked nervously.

"Could be one of the kids, could be almost anybody," Baxter whispered.

"You open the door and I'll get ready over at the side in case it's trouble. You better hope it's just one of your boys, Baxter. Marcel and me don't like trouble."

CHAPTER

Baxter slammed the inside lock on the metal door and quickly pushed the door up. He hunched up his powerful shoulders getting ready to meet anyone who might try to get past him.

It was only Robert's father.

"Crazy Phil, what a pleasure to have you come for a visit. Does this mean you've changed your mind about working for us?" Baxter smiled at the old man.

"You rat, it only means I've got a message to give you. I've never done any deals with men like you and I'm not going to start now. Step outside here and we'll talk for a minute," Phil said.

"So this is the guy who's causing all the trouble," Frank said as he stepped out of the shadows. "From all I heard about you, Crazy Phil, I was expecting someone a little bigger and a little smarter."

"My uncle used to say that you could go a long way if you were smart, but even further if you were honest. He ended up by making a fortune," Phil said, smiling at the two men. "You two should follow his advice and get out of this business while you still can. I won't give up, you know. I won't sell the junkyard and I won't work with you. I'm just going to sit in my shop with one eye on the yard and the other on my telephone. If any of your men step across that fence, I'll phone the police," Phil said, staring at the men.

"Come on, Crazy Phil, be reasonable," Frank said, taking a step toward the old man.

"I am reasonable. I've never been so reasonable in my whole crazy life. You guys should sell this warehouse and get into some honest business. Go sell underwear or open a bookstore or. . . ."

Frank jumped at Crazy Phil before the old man could finish. Phil tried to punch at Frank as the man came near him, but he missed and lost his balance. Frank quickly twisted the old man's arm and made him fall down onto the gravel driveway. Frank worked hard to pin Phil down. The old man kept twisting and squirming from his grip.

"Come on, Baxter, give me a hand," Frank shouted.

Baxter came running over to help. He grabbed Crazy Phil around the neck and bent the old man's arm behind his back. Phil kept struggling in Baxter's powerful grip, but it was useless.

Once the old man was trapped Frank got up and tried to catch his breath. "Who would ever think the old guy was such a fighter, huh? Look, Crazy Phil, you probably think you're being some sort of hero, but you're just being stupid. We're not going to kill you. It's a lot easier for us to kill the things that are important to you."

"You already killed my dogs, you rats."

"But we haven't even touched your

son, have we," Frank said with a smile.

"You wouldn't dare lay a finger on him," Crazy Phil said and started twisting so hard that Baxter almost lost his grip.

"Not yet, we won't. First we'll give you a personal example of what could happen to him."

Frank got ready to strike at Crazy Phil as the old man struggled in Baxter's powerful headlock. He sent one punch to Phil's stomach before he was surprised by a voice right behind him.

"Stop it and let him up."

Frank wheeled around to see Dave standing with a bottle of acid in one hand. Frank took one look at the acid and then backed away from Crazy Phil.

"Robert, you head over to the junkyard and call the police while I hold these guys here," Dave said. He waited until Robert had started off and then spoke to the short man who still held Crazy Phil.

"Baxter, I expected to see you again but not like this—now let the old man go."

Baxter relaxed his grip on Crazy Phil

so the old man could get free. He kept on staring at Dave trying to figure out where he had seen him before.

"You're the kid who was gonna buy the Corvette."

"Yeah, I had talked myself into going along with you guys until I saw what was happening here. It's one thing to be selling stolen cars, it's another thing to be beating up old men," Dave said.

"Dave, when are you going to see that it's really all the same," Crazy Phil broke in as he struggled to his feet. His voice cracked and he began to cough.

"Are you going to be O.K., Phil?" Dave asked. He took his eyes off the two men to look over at Robert's father. That was enough time for Baxter to rush him.

"Stay back," Dave yelled. His cry came too late as Baxter's shoulder caught him right in the stomach. The bottle of acid fell out of Dave's hand and spilled uselessly on the ground.

Dave lost his balance from the force of Baxter's blow and fell backward onto the gravel. A second later, Baxter was on him and Dave was trapped in a headlock.

Crazy Phil got in the fight and tried

to pull Baxter off. The old man used all the strength he had left, but he was getting nowhere. Frank ran over and clobbered the old man in the side of the head. The blow sent Crazy Phil falling to the ground and left Dave at the mercy of the two men.

"What happened to that other kid?" Frank shouted.

"He went to the junkyard to ... look at that!"

Baxter's words were cut off by the sound of the junkyard fence crashing down.

CHAPTER
10

Robert heard the sound of the fight just after he got inside the junkyard fence. He turned in time to see Frank hitting his father. He knew right then that he'd never make it to the office in time.

Robert was trying to figure out what he could do when he saw the Blue Goose parked in front of him. A second later, he was inside the cab of the truck and racing the engine. He threw off the parking brake and the truck raced toward the junkyard fence.

Robert didn't really know what would happen when the truck hit the fence. He just hoped that the old wooden slats would give way.

He was right. With the cracking sound of smashing wood pounding in his ears, the truck broke through the fence and raced toward the men at the warehouse.

Robert had little time to decide what to do once he got past the fence. He saw his father lying on the ground. Baxter and Frank were holding Dave on the gravel driveway.

Robert figured the sound of him crashing through the fence had scared the two men. He hoped he could use the Blue Goose to scare them even more.

Robert pulled out the throttle to race the engine and steered the pickup right at the two men. He knew he'd have to cut away at the last minute or risk hitting Dave and his father. He only hoped the surprise might give them all the break they needed.

His plan worked better than he expected. Frank stood up as the old pickup rushed toward him. He froze for a second and then ran wildly down the driveway.

Baxter saw what he was doing and shouted after him, "Don't be stupid!"

Dave used this chance to twist out of Baxter's grip. He rolled away and was on his feet in an instant.

Robert saw Frank dart away from the others so he steered the Blue Goose after the man. As he turned, the truck skidded on the gravel. Robert slammed the steering wheel to the left to cut the skid. He eased up on the throttle for a bit and then headed after Frank again.

Robert saw that Frank was running wildly back and forth. His zig-zag path made him hard to follow with the truck. Robert had no idea what to do next. He didn't want to hit Frank with the truck, but he had to keep him from running back toward Dave and Crazy Phil.

Frank had almost made it to the end of the driveway when his feet slipped on the gravel. He rolled over on the ground and watched the pickup speed toward him.

Robert slammed on the parking brake to lock the rear wheels of the pickup. The truck went into a skid toward the left. Robert steered into it, trying hard to

control the speeding truck.

A cloud of dust came up from the gravel and Robert couldn't see outside the cab. He steered wildly, madly, unsure where he was going or what would happen next.

Robert heard a dull thud come from the back of the truck just before the old Ford came to a stop. When the dust cleared enough to see, Robert saw Frank down on the gravel. The man was doubled over and moaning in pain.

The truck had turned right around in the skid and was now facing back toward the warehouse door. Robert looked up to see Dave and Baxter facing off in front of the warehouse. Robert's father was getting up from the ground and stag-gering over into the warehouse.

Once again, Robert wasn't quite sure what to do. He decided to trust to luck and the Blue Goose. He ground the starter until the stalled engine caught and then raced back toward Dave and Baxter.

Baxter took one look at the truck speeding toward him and the figure of Frank on the ground. Then he bolted toward the hole in the junkyard fence.

Robert watched Baxter run toward the fence. He brought the truck up beside Dave and slowed to a stop.

"Let me hang on here and we'll go get him," Dave shouted.

Dave climbed onto the running board of the truck. He held tightly to the large side-view mirror as Robert raced the Blue Goose toward the hole in the fence.

Baxter ran between the wrecked Pinto and the back end of a Pontiac in a space where the truck couldn't reach him. He turned and waited for Dave and Robert to come after him.

"Pull up beside the Pinto. Keep up your speed so I can jump him," Dave yelled through the window.

Robert raced the truck over the broken fence boards and back into the junkyard before pushing in the throttle. The Blue Goose began to slow down as Robert brought it closer to where Baxter was waiting. At the last minute, he turned quickly to the right. Dave jumped off the running board and right into Baxter.

The truck crashed into the Pinto just

as Dave jumped on Baxter. The speed of the truck worked with Dave's jump to push Baxter off his feet. Baxter flew backward and hit his head against the side of the Pinto.

"Is he hurt much?" Robert shouted as he cut the truck's engine.

Dave bent down over Baxter's body and saw that the powerful man's chest was still moving up and down.

"I think he's just had the wind knocked out of him," Dave said.

Robert and Dave had just started to catch their breath when they heard someone groaning on the other side of the fence. They looked up and saw Crazy Phil stumble into the junkyard.

"Oohah. I haven't felt so bad since I got into a fight with the back end of a model A Ford in a downtown parking lot. I lost the fight but I sure gave the car's bumper a piece of my mind," Crazy Phil said.

"Are you O.K., dad?" Robert asked.

"Of course I'm not O.K.," Crazy Phil coughed. "That midget wrestler over there has spent the last half hour trying to pound my body into ground beef. And

your friend Dave was so clumsy with that acid bottle that I'm lucky to have any skin left."

Robert and Dave had to laugh when Crazy Phil turned around and showed them holes the acid had made in his overalls.

"I'd better get out of these before the acid eats through my underwear. I'd be so hole-y I could end up in church," Phil said smiling.

"We rescue you from a beating, break up an entire stolen car gang, and all you can do is make lousy jokes," Robert said.

"I can do more than that," Phil answered.

"What?"

"I can call the police before Baxter wakes up. If I don't hurry up, we'll have a lot more to worry about than just holes in my underwear," Phil said as he walked off toward the shop.

Books in this series:

BURN OUT
Bob and Chewie have a plan to catch the firebugs on Maple Street. The plan seems good at first. But when it backfires they get trapped in the basement of a burning house.

DEAD ON
What is making the strange sound in the hall outside Larry's room? It can't be a ghost. Larry does not believe in ghosts. But someone — or something — keeps leading him to the attic of the old house.

DIRT BIKE
Twenty cycles roar out of the start chute. Randy races toward the first turn on his yellow dirt bike. He looks over at Bozo and grits his teeth. Only one of them can come out the winner.

DOPE DEAL
Brian has to face a lot of problems. He gets busted by the cops, has to move back home and beats up his own brother. But his biggest problem comes when he takes on a whole motorcycle gang.

FAIR PLAY
When Andy Singh asks Carol to the party, she couldn't care less whether his skin is black or white. But her old boyfriend cares far too much. His jealousy and hate lead to a night of danger on the icy streets of Windsor.

HOT CARS

At first Robert doesn't know who is killing his dogs or wrecking his father's truck. When he gets trapped by a stolen-car gang, the answer almost kills him.

NO WAY

Pete only wants to show the others how brave he is. But his plan for the perfect rip-off falls apart. He ends up in trouble with the law. Now his old gang wants him to steal from the only people he really cares about.

RUNAWAY

Kathy wishes she were a goldfish. She has some good reasons — her father gets drunk and beats her, her best friend drives her crazy and her boyfriend wants to get too friendly. Will she be better off if she runs away?